This Little Tiger book
belongs to:

_____

_____

_____

TOGE

LITTLE TIGER PRESS LTD,
an imprint of the Little Tiger Group
1 Coda Studios, 189 Munster Road,
London SW6 6AW
Imported into the EEA by
Penguin Random House Ireland,
Morrison Chambers, 32 Nassau Street,
Dublin D02 YH68
www.littletiger.co.uk

First published in Great Britain 2020
This edition published 2021

Text and illustrations copyright © Jane Chapman 2020
Visit Jane Chapman at www.janekchapman.com
Jane Chapman has asserted her right to be identified
as the author and illustrator of this work under the Copyright,
Designs and Patents Act, 1988
A CIP catalogue record for this book is available from
the British Library • All rights reserved

ISBN 978-1-78881-680-9
Printed in China
LTP/1800/3739/0321

10 9 8 7 6 5 4 3 2 1

The Forest Stewardship Council® (FSC®) is an international, non-governmental
organisation dedicated to promoting responsible management of the world's forests.
FSC® operates a system of forest certification and product labelling that allows
consumers to identify wood and wood-based products from well-managed forests.

For more information about the FSC®, please visit their website at www.fsc.org

FSC
www.fsc.org
MIX
Paper from
responsible sources
FSC® C020056

THER

Jane Chapman

LiTTLE TiGER
LONDON

Hidden under shady leaves,
a tiny face peeps out.
Silent. Alone.

Outside,
the world
is strange
and shadowy.

But rain clouds bring

sweet water,

wind brings the
smell of food . . .

and something else.
Something new,
something BIG.
Something . . .

. . . . scary.

But behind this
fearsome face is kindness.
A soft hand.

A friend who will

share their feast . . .

Who will bring
a smile . . .

And make the world

feel safe again . . .

Even magical.

Some days the world may still seem full of shadows.

But that **friend**

will be there

to share

adventures . . .

and find
happiness . . .

Together.